ALL YOU NE

A Lover's Guide

By Sally Humphreys & Geraint Humphreys

First published in 2010. A catalogue record for this book is available from the British Library

ISBN 978-1-844259-51-9

Published by Haynes Publishing, Sparkford, Yeovil, Somerset BA22 7JJ, UK

Tel: 01963 442030 Fax: 01963 440001 Int. tel: +44 1963 442030 Int. fax: +44 1963 440001

E-mail: sales@haynes.co.uk Website: www.haynes.co.uk

Haynes North America Inc., 861 Lawrence Drive, Newbury Park, California 91320, USA

Series Editor: Richard Havers

Creative Director: Kevin Gardner

Design and Artwork: David Wildish

Special thanks to: Michael Throne

Additional thanks to: Adam Vaigncourt-Strallen

The Bell Lomax Moreton Agency

Packaged for Haynes by Green Umbrella Publishing

Printed and bound in Britain by JF Print Ltd., Sparkford. Somerset

To My Wonderful Wife Natasha

From Your Loving Husband Edward

on our first Wedding Anniversary
with all my love now & forever
xxxxx

Introduction

Welcome to *All You Need Is Love*, a heart-warming collection of love-related facts and figures, quotes and poetry, pictures and stories, heartbreak and happiness – all of which combine to paint a picture of the complex, contrary and frankly enormous topic that is love.

Love dominates our daily lives in a myriad of ways; it's the front page of every newspaper, the story in a soap opera, the theme of a song. It's what puts a spring in our step or makes us hide under the covers (in more ways than one...) It's kissing a partner or celebrating being single. Living in the moment or revelling in the memories.

It's not just a noun or a verb – it's both, of course. It's a philosophy, a gift, even a weapon. It can be a tiny token of affection or the grandest of gestures, an enriching but equally destructive force.

Imagine for a moment that poets, musicians, painters and filmmakers didn't have love as a source of inspiration. Where would we be then? Well – it wouldn't take long to reach the end of this book, that's for sure.

So take a moment to relax and enjoy this collection of love trivia – it really is all you need.

“Two **souls** with but a single **thought**, two **hearts** that **beat** as one.”

John Keats

The Definition of Love

Love [pronounced: luhv]

– noun

1. A deeply tender, passionate fondness for another person.
2. A feeling of profound affection, as for a parent, child or friend.
3. Sexual passion or longing.
4. A person towards whom love is felt; beloved person.
5. Used as a term of endearment when addressing another: would you like a cup of tea, love?
6. A love affair; an intensely romantic incident.
7. Sexual intercourse.
8. A personification of sexual affection: e.g. Cupid.
9. Concern for the well-being of others: loving one's neighbour.
10. Tendency, enthusiasm, or liking of anything: his love for the ladies.
11. The object or thing so liked: he was her great love.
12. In tennis, a score of nothing.

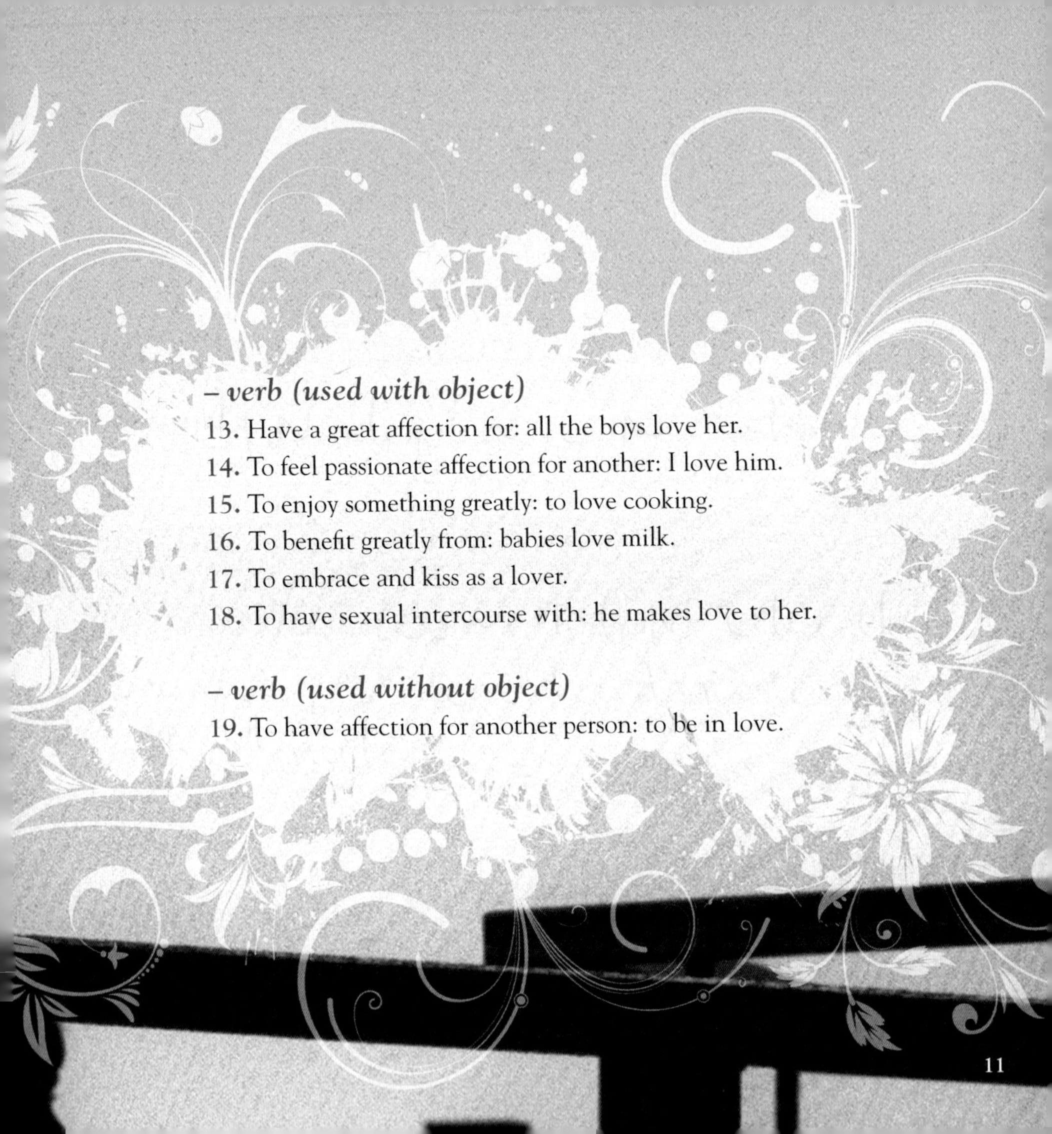

– verb (used with object)

13. Have a great affection for: all the boys love her.
14. To feel passionate affection for another: I love him.
15. To enjoy something greatly: to love cooking.
16. To benefit greatly from: babies love milk.
17. To embrace and kiss as a lover.
18. To have sexual intercourse with: he makes love to her.

– verb (used without object)

19. To have affection for another person: to be in love.

Cupid, Draw Back Your Bow...

The image of Cupid is one we automatically associate with love, even if we are unaware of his place in Roman mythology. One glimpse of the famous cherub is enough to make us recall the ability of his golden arrows, which famously inspire love between two people. So where does the story come from?

Cupid – or, to use his Latin name, Amor – was the son of Venus (goddess of love) and Mars (god of war). The archery skills, one presumes, must have been passed down from his father's side.

Venus, according to myth, became jealous of Princess Psyche, a mortal contender for the affections of the people. So enraptured were Psyche's subjects that they soon forgot to worship Venus, who subsequently ordered Cupid to make Psyche fall in love with the most unpleasant thing on earth.

Cupid, however, did not honour his mother's wishes; he too had been distracted by Psyche's beauty. This momentary lapse in concentration caused him to drop an arrow, piercing his own foot and causing him to fall completely for the princess.

Meanwhile, an oracle revealed that Psyche's beauty was not meant for mortal men, so she was left on a mountainside where the Zephyrus wind delivered her promised bridegroom, Cupid. Though Psyche was unaware of his identity, the marriage was consummated.

Despite Cupid's insistence that Psyche must not see him, her sisters tricked her into looking. His identity revealed, Cupid fled, leaving Psyche to trick her sisters as punishment. Believing that Cupid wished to marry *them*, each sister waited on the mountainside for him, eventually falling to their deaths.

Psyche was then told to consult Venus for advice, but the still-bitter Venus sent her on a wild goose chase. Despite her best efforts, Psyche survived this fiendish ploy, and the council of gods decreed that Psyche and Cupid should marry.

Psyche, now granted immortality, forgave Venus and bore Cupid a daughter, Voluptas, the goddess of sensual pleasures.

Just remember all that, next time you see Cupid on a Valentine's Day card…

“ **Love** looks not with the
eyes, but with the **mind**,
And therefore is wing’d
Cupid painted **blind**. ”

William Shakespeare

The Chemistry of Love

The heart is the symbol most commonly associated with love – but why does it beat that little bit faster when we fall in love?

The Chemistry of Love

If we look to science for an answer, we find the answer lies with the brain, which releases certain chemicals into our system as we **react to the three stages of love: lust, attraction and attachment.**

The Chemistry of Love

When we get that unmistakeable urge to find a partner, it is lust that drives us. Unsurprisingly, this sensation is induced by our sex hormones, testosterone and oestrogen, and is regarded as a mammalian instinct. Like eating and drinking, we naturally have an urge to mate – but this stage is tricky, as our brains may cause us to stop thinking rationally and therefore pursue the "wrong" type of partner. However, this "lust" is short-lived, and quickly turns into "attraction".

Attraction is what might be considered the "falling in love stage", namely, the period in which we consider committing to one partner. At this point, the brain releases an amphetamine-like combination of chemicals (pheromones, dopamine, norepinephrine, and serotonin) that stimulate the brain's pleasure centre, resulting in increased heart rate, blissful feelings and even loss of appetite and sleep.

The Chemistry of Love

As with lust, the attraction period has a limited shelf life. Therefore, in order for relationships to survive on a long-term basis, there is one final stage: "attachment".

From a scientific point of view, attachment is associated with higher levels of the chemicals oxytocin and vasopressin, which do not appear in the same quantities during short-term relationships. It is these, coupled with carefully used endorphins, which keep us happy even though we no longer see our partner through rose-tinted spectacles. External factors such as marriage and family also help to motivate prolonged attachment.

Unfortunately for some, getting past the endorphin rush of the lust and attraction stages can be difficult; these people are known as "love junkies" because they continue to seek new highs rather than settle down. Be warned, though – if a "love junkie" tries to force him or herself into a long-term relationship, they are more likely to stray… so if you have a happy, long-lasting relationship, now you know why people say you have "great chemistry"!

“There is no **instinct** like that of the **heart**.”

Lord Byron

Ways to say I love you...

There are many ways to remind your partner how you feel – why not show how much you care with some of these suggestions?

- Wake up first and surprise them with breakfast in bed. If you haven't got time for that – or the necessary ingredients – a cup of tea or coffee still works wonders.

- Compile a mixed CD of their favourite songs, plus ones that have special relevance to your relationship.

- Surprise them with a romantic night out. Don't forget to foot the bill!

- Without prompting, present them with a DVD you know they will like.
- Re-create your first date.
- Make biscuits and ice them with personalized messages.
- Send flowers for no reason – but don't forget to say who they're from…
- Post them a love letter (no cheating with email, please).
- Offer a massage or foot rub – without expecting one in return.
- Do ALL the household chores ready for their arrival back home.

VALENTINE WAY.

“**Anyone** can catch your **eye**, but it takes **someone special** to catch your **heart**.”

Author unknown

Valentine's Day

Valentine's Day: the most romantic day of the year, or an increasingly commercialized "holiday" designed to make us part with our cash?

While there is undoubtedly some truth in the latter description, Valentine's Day – or St Valentine's Day, as it is also known – is generally considered one of the first holidays to be marked by the exchange of written greetings, and the move from handmade to purchased designs happened well over a century ago.

The true origins of the practice remain unclear, but some believe it can be traced to the third century, when Emperor Claudius II jailed St Valentine for refusing to renounce his Christian beliefs. While languishing behind bars, Valentine is said to have slipped a love-note to the jailer's daughter, signed "from your Valentine". This tale has given rise to the popular notion of St Valentine being the patron saint of lovers.

Other theories associate Valentine's Day with the Roman fertility festival Lupercalia, a less-than-romantic event that included the whipping of young women in a bid to boost their fertility. They probably would have preferred a card and a

box of Milk Tray…

Although the oldest surviving Valentine dates back to 1415, the so-called "golden age" of commercially produced cards is said to have been the late 1800s. Handmade efforts by the English were overtaken by designs featuring the now traditional verse of the "roses are red, violets are blue" variety. High-end cards printed on premium paper and wrapped in ribbon or lace started to surface. Inspired by these lucrative efforts, American entrepreneur Esther Howland set up her own Valentine's card company in 1847, in Worcester, Massachusetts. The exchanging of handmade love notes already existed in America, but Howard's products quickly established themselves as the norm.

Fast forward to the present day and over one billion Valentine's Day cards are sent annually – suggesting that the "golden age" is actually right now. And for any ladies who think men do not make enough effort on 14th February, know this: research shows that, on average, men spend twice as much as women when it comes to Valentine's Day!

Sonnet 18

"Shall I compare thee to a summer's day?
Thou art more lovely and more temperate:
Rough winds do shake the darling buds of May,
And summer's lease hath all too short a date:
Sometime too hot the eye of heaven shines,
And often is his gold complexion dimm'd;
And every fair from fair sometime declines,
By chance or nature's changing course untrimm'd;
But thy eternal summer shall not fade
Nor lose possession of that fair thou ow'st;
Nor shall Death brag thou wander'st in his shade,
When in eternal lines to time thou grow'st:
So long as men can breathe or eyes can see,
So long lives this and this gives life to thee."

William Shakespeare

Great Romances of Our Time

Edward VIII and Mrs Wallis Simpson

The story of how King Edward VIII chose to give up the British throne in order to marry an American socialite – the already married *and* once-divorced Wallis Simpson – was a scandal that rocked the monarchy.

When Edward made the decision to abdicate in December 1936, he revealed, "I have found it impossible to carry the heavy burden of responsibility and to discharge my duties as King as I would wish to do without the help and support of the woman I love."

By mid-1937, sufficient time had passed for Simpson to be granted a decree absolute in her second divorce, and the pair married in France. No members of the monarchy were present, and although former King Edward now went by the title of His Royal Highness the Duke of Windsor, Simpson had to make do with the straight forward title of Duchess of Windsor. Simpson felt so bitterly snubbed by Britain that she once remarked, "I hate this country. I shall hate it to my grave."

Although relations never truly thawed between Simpson and the monarchy, she eventually travelled to England and was permitted to stay at Buckingham Palace for Edward's funeral in 1972.

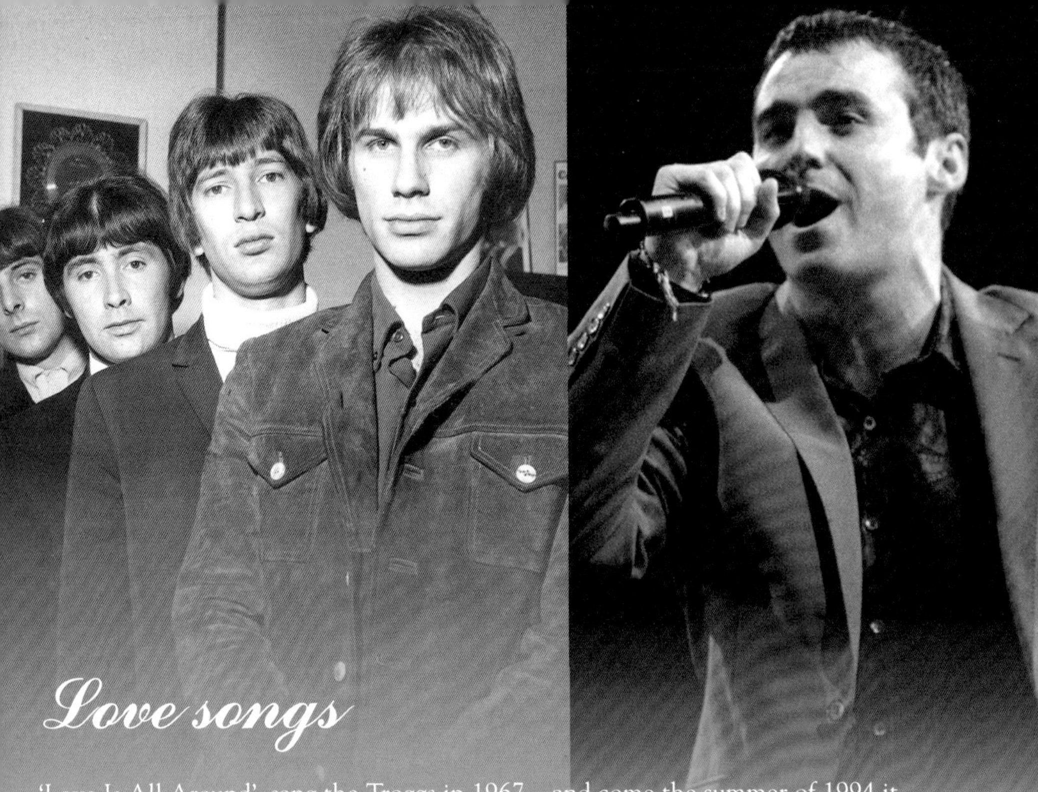

Love songs

'Love Is All Around', sang the Troggs in 1967 – and come the summer of 1994 it really was all around thanks to Wet Wet Wet's ubiquitous cover. The Scottish band spent 15 weeks at the top after their interpretation was used in the ultimate '90s rom-com, *Four Weddings and a Funeral*. Evidently, love songs and love stories are a winning combination – indeed, love in some form seems to be the inspiration behind almost every song we hear on the radio.

Love songs

Throughout this book you will find 50 of the biggest and best love songs of all time – which is your favourite?

Whitney Houston – 'I Will Always Love You'

Composer Dolly Parton first released this song in 1974. Whitney's arguably definitive version came out in 1992.

Righteous Brothers – 'Unchained Melody'

Said to be one of the most recorded songs in history, with over 500 versions known to exist.

Céline Dion – 'My Heart Will Go On'

The world's bestselling single in 1998, and one of the biggest selling songs of all time.

Bryan Adams – 'Everything I Do (I Do It For You)'

Topped the charts in over 30 countries.

Bangles – 'Eternal Flame'

Topped the UK charts twice – once in 1989 and again in 2001 when Atomic Kitten's cover rose to the top.

Elvis Presley – 'Love Me Tender'

The movie *Love Me Tender* was originally titled *The Reno Brothers* but was hastily altered to cash in on the popularity of this song from the soundtrack.

Roxette – 'It Must Have Been Love'

This song appeared on the *Pretty Woman* soundtrack in 1990 but didn't appear on a Roxette album until their hits collection *Don't Bore Us, Get To The Chorus* was released.

Aerosmith – 'I Don't Want To Miss A Thing'

Taken from the *Armageddon* soundtrack, 'I Don't Want To Miss A Thing' was the first Aerosmith song to debut at number 1; 28 years into the band's career.

Lionel Richie (with Diana Ross) – 'Endless Love'

Luther Vandross and Mariah Carey covered this 1981 classic in 1995.

Meat Loaf – 'I'd Do Anything For Love (But I Won't Do That)'

Many people incorrectly believe that the nature of "that" is never revealed, but the lyrics do see Meatloaf responding "I won't do that" to the female singer's assertion that "You'll see that it's time to move on" and "You'll be screwing around".

Blind Dates

Many single people dread the idea of going on a blind date arranged by a well-meaning friend, colleague or family member – but the rise of Internet dating suggests people are increasingly willing to at least engineer their own, semi-blind dates.

With applications doubling in January, the post-Christmas and New Year "slump" is traditionally the peak time for signing up to dating sites – so bear that in mind if you want to increase your chances of finding love…

If all else fails, perhaps Cilla Black can be coaxed out of retirement – her *Blind Date* show regularly drew audiences of up to 14 million in the late eighties, and even won her a BAFTA award. Cilla's strike-rate wasn't spectacular, admittedly – but at least everybody had fun, and there were a few weddings along the way. Who could forget "that hat" moment? What a lorra lorra laughs that was!

KIRKPATRICK FLEMING 3¼ M
GRETNA GREEN
CARLISLE 9½ M

Gretna Green

Gretna Green: two words to strike fear into the heart of every parent – the reason being, of course, Gretna Green's history of "runaway marriages".

This tradition came into being in 1753, when Lord Hardwicke's Marriage Act decreed that parental consent had to be given at English weddings if both parties were under 21. However, no such law applied in Scotland, where boys of 14 and girls of 12 could still marry without parental consent (ages which rose to 16 in 1929). As a result, many impatient young lovers began eloping to Scotland to exchange their vows.

Back then, the first place encountered by visiting couples was Gretna Green's Old Blacksmiths, and as Scottish law allowed for "irregular marriages", almost anyone could officiate at a wedding. This led to the term "anvil priests", and to this day all Gretna marriages are performed over a symbolic Blacksmith's anvil.

Gretna has become one of the most popular wedding destinations in the world, with over 5,000 ceremonies a year. As well as this, one in six Scottish weddings are said to take place there.

A Red, Red Rose

O my luve's like a red, red rose,
That's newly sprung in June;
O my luve's like the melodie
That's sweetly play'd in tune.

As fair art thou, my bonie lass,
So deep in luve am I,
And I will luve thee still, my Dear,
Till a' the seas gang dry.

Till a' the seas gang dry, my Dear,
And the rocks melt wi' the sun:
I will luve thee still, my Dear,
While the sands o' life shall run.

And fare thee weel, my only Luve,
And fare thee weel a while!
And I will come again, my Luve,
Tho' it were ten thousand mile!

Robert Burns

Weddings

Weddings are big business. Even a recession has failed to reduce the amount of couples lining up to say "I do" – in fact it's quite the opposite: recent figures indicate that UK wedding ceremonies actually rose in number during 2008 and 2009, a trend attributed to a need for stability during a period of financial uncertainty. The last similar "spike" came in 1940, when the outbreak of war resulted in thousands flocking to make their way down the aisle.

Despite this increase, wedding planners have noted a marked change in spending habits. More couples are sticking to a tight budget, and demand for winter services – up to 50% cheaper than summer bashes – has also rocketed.

It hasn't always been this way. American wedding statistics for 2005–2006 indicate that 2.16 million weddings generated $86 billion in revenue, and that the inclusion of an average bride's spending six months before and six months after the wedding would have brought the total to a whopping $120 billion. That's not including gifts and honeymoons, by the way!

Zephyr 6
KVX 318C
JUST
MARRIED

Fascinating UK wedding facts

- The average engagement is 18 months.
- The average wedding costs £20,000, with £520 spent on flowers.
- The average bride is 29, while her groom is 31.
- 95% of couples won't sign a pre-nuptial agreement.
- 12% of brides keep their own surname after marriage.
- The average engagement ring costs £2,200.
- 61% of brides choose their own engagement ring.
- 97% of grooms wear a wedding ring.
- 45% of couples chose a religious ceremony.
- Brides paid an average of £1,200 for their dress.
- Couples spend approximately £4,000 on their honeymoon.

The wedding dance: a unique, never-to-be-forgotten opportunity for newlyweds to demonstrate their natural chemistry together, or a nerve-wracking and potentially embarrassing tradition, ideally dispensed with as quickly as possible so the rest of the reception can be enjoyed in a stress-free manner?

The fact that more and more couples are opting for dancing lessons in advance of their big day suggests the answer lies somewhere between these two viewpoints – some want their first dance to impress, while others simply want to ensure they don't tread on their partner's toes or go flying across an otherwise empty dance floor.

Perhaps that's why so many people pick slow songs… here are 10 of the most popular songs used for that all-important "first dance":

Aerosmith – 'Don't Wanna Miss A Thing'

Bryan Adams – 'Everything I Do (I Do It For You)'

Eric Clapton – 'Wonderful Tonight'

Lonestar – 'Amazed'

Shania Twain – 'You're Still The One'

James Blunt – 'You're Beautiful'

Savage Garden – 'Truly Madly Deeply'

Robbie Williams – 'Angels'

Whitney Houston – 'I Will Always Love You'

Elvis Presley – 'Can't Help Falling In Love'

Civil Partnerships

The UK's first civil partnership took place on 19th December 2005, when Shannon Sickles and Grainne Close exchanged vows at Belfast City Hall, Northern Ireland.

Speaking beforehand, Ms Close said: "For us, this is about making a choice to have our civil rights acknowledged, and respected and protected as any human being. We could not be here without the hard work of many queer activists and individuals from the queer community and we feel very privileged and blessed to be here doing this."

Her partner Ms Sickles added, "This is for all the people who went before us, and this is for protection."

In the nine months that followed, more than 15,000 couples took advantage of the new Civil Partnership Act, which provided same-sex couples with similar rights to married couples.

The first high-profile couple to take advantage of the Act were Sir Elton John and David Furnish, who wed less than a week after the new law came into place. Celebrity guests at their union included Ringo Starr, Liz Hurley, Cilla Black, Donatella Versace, Claudia Schiffer, Sam Taylor-Wood, James Blunt, Greg Rusedski, Jamie Cullum, Michael Vaughan, the Osbournes and the Beckhams. Speaking at the event, singer Lulu noted: "This could only happen for Elton."

Great Romances of Our Time

Spencer Tracy and Katharine Hepburn

Spencer Tracy and Katharine Hepburn felt an immediate attraction when meeting on the set of 1942's *Woman of the Year*, and so began one of Hollywood's most famous affairs. However, the relationship went unacknowledged for many years, mainly because Catholic Tracy refused to divorce his estranged wife, Louise.

Tracy and Hepburn worked together many times – appearing in *Keeper of the Flame* (1942), *Adam's Rib* (1949), *Pat and Mike* (1952), *Desk Set* (1957) and *Guess Who's Coming to Dinner* (1967) – and it is said the warring couples they portrayed were a mirror of their actual relationship. Indeed, Hepburn's 1994 obituary in *The Daily Telegraph* read: "Hepburn and Spencer Tracy were at their most seductive when their verbal fencing was sharpest; it was hard to say whether they delighted more in the battle or in each other."

Although Hepburn and Tracy never lived together, she cared for him in his final days after a lifetime of binge-drinking finally caught up with him. Upon meeting his wife, Hepburn is said to have wondered aloud if they could have been friends, only for Mrs Tracy to respond, "Well, yes – but you see, I thought you were only a rumour."

Puppy Love

Puppy love: a term referring to a crush, or the giddy thrill of young love, both of which resemble the hopeless adoration most people feel when presented with a puppy. Who can say no to those big paws and even bigger eyes?

Dogs are said to be man's best friend, but who is to say "puppy love" shouldn't be renamed in honour of kittens, bunnies, hedgehogs, chicks, fawns, otters, pandas… the list is seemingly endless!

Make no mistake about it, animals – especially baby ones – are capable of melting even the hardest of hearts.

PUPPY LOVE
FOR SALE.

Love is patient and kind;
love is not jealous or boastful;
it is not arrogant or rude
Love does not insist on its own way;
it is not irritable or resentful;
it does not rejoice at wrong,
but rejoices in the right.
Love bears all things;
believes all things;
hopes all things;
endures all things.

1 Corinthians 13:4

Love Quiz 1

Can you match these famous lovers?

- Prince Albert
- Romeo
- Mark Antony
- Lancelot
- Tristan
- Melanie Griffith
- Orpheus
- Napoleon
- Posh
- Odysseus
- Rhett Butler
- Rochester
- Pyramus
- Judy Finnigan
- Mr Darcy
- Shah Jahan
- Pierre Curie
- Helen
- John Lennon

- Marie Curie
- Scarlett O'Hara
- Cleopatra
- Becks
- Isolde
- Antonio Banderas
- Eurydice
- Josephine
- Juliet
- Yoko Ono
- Penelope
- Jane Eyre
- Thisbe
- Guinevere
- Richard Madeley
- Elizabeth Bennett
- Mumtaz Mahal
- Queen Victoria
- Paris

Answers on page 174

Different Types of Love

To brand love a complex topic is something of an understatement – there are many types, and all can change over time. Here are just a few examples…

Passionate Love

Passionate love is the intense desire for physical union with another. It is related to beauty and our strong physical and emotional reaction to it. Be warned though, the reciprocation of passionate love may lead to feelings of fulfilment, but this is notoriously short lived.

Romantic Love

Although some consider romantic love to be a mix of emotional and physical desire, it is more commonly associated with the expression of love through words and actions. By behaving in this way, we truly convey our deep attachment to and enthusiasm for another person.

Familial Love

Familial love is the natural bond enjoyed by those connected by blood or shared lineage. This type of love is noted for being selfless, mutual and unconditional.

Platonic Love

Platonic love refers to relationships in which people are friendly and affectionate but not sexually intimate with one another.

Jealous Love

Jealousy differs from envy in that it refers to the fear of losing what we have, as opposed to desiring what we do not have. If we fear the loss of a loved one to another, we become angry, suspicious, irrational and uncertain.

It's not all bad news though – some scientists claim there is a link between jealousy and increased sexual function and satisfaction.

Unrequited Love

Unrequited love is the painful yearning for someone who does not feel the same way. The object of affection is frequently unaware of the admirer's deep feelings.

“‘Tis better to
have **loved** and **lost**
Than never to have
loved at all.”

Alfred Tennyson

The Kama Sutra

The Mallanãga Vãtsyãyana's *Kama Sutra* is an ancient Indian text concerning *dharma* (virtue); *artha* (prosperity); *Kama* (love/aesthetic and sensual pleasure); and *moksha* (death and rebirth).

Vãtsyãyana's general outlook is that childhood is for learning to make a living (*artha*), while youth is the time for pleasure (*kama*). Older generations should pursue virtue (*dharma*) in order to avoid the cycle of death and rebirth (*moksha*).

Despite the philosophical nature of the work, the sensual pleasures detailed within – 64 sexual acts across 10 chapters – are surely its best-known aspect.

The text is divided into 36 chapters across the following 7 sections:

1. The introduction (concerning aims and priorities of life and the acquisition of knowledge): 5 chapters.

2. The aforementioned topic of sexual union (concerning erotic stimulation/foreplay via embracing, caressing, kisses, marking with nails, biting and marking with teeth, positions, slapping by hand, moaning, oral sex, and climax): 10 chapters.

3. The acquisition of a wife (how to "get the girl", relax her, commit to her and marry her): 5 chapters.

4&5. The conduct of wives (concerning the behaviour of woman and man, becoming acquainted, the behaviour of women): 8 chapters.

6. Courtesans (concerning the advice of assistants regarding choice of lovers, ways of making money and remaining on good terms with former lovers): 6 chapters.

7. Attracting others to one's self (maintaining appearance to remain physically attractive): 2 chapters.

And before you ask – yes, the illustrations can be found in section two.

Great Romances of Our Time

Richard Burton and Elizabeth Taylor

Richard Burton and Elizabeth Taylor married in 1963, 10 years after Burton first remarked: "Her breasts would topple empires before they withered... [Taylor] was the most sullen, uncommunicative and beautiful woman I had ever seen." In 1962, the two stars began an on-set affair that scandalized the tabloids and led to a decadent and volatile marriage.

Taylor once described their partnership as being "like chicken feathers to tar", and by 1973 the party was over. Despite their divorce, Taylor and Burton were inexorably drawn back to each other and remarried in 1975, a disastrous reunion lasting just four months.

When Burton died in 1984, his wife barred Taylor from attending the funeral, but legend has it that Taylor received the most condolences.

Love's Philosophy

The fountains mingle with the river
And the rivers with the ocean,
The winds of heaven mix for ever
With a sweet emotion;
Nothing in the world is single,
All things by a law divine
In one another's being mingle –
Why not I with thine?

See the mountains kiss high heaven
And the waves clasp one another;
No sister-flower would be forgiven
If it disdain'd its brother:

And the sunlight clasps the earth,
And the moonbeams kiss the sea –
What are all these kissings worth,
If thou kiss not me?

Percy Bysshe Shelley

Love Music Facts

Shania Twain 'You're Still The One'

Shania Twain's 1997 ode to then partner Mutt Lange 'You're Still The One' sold over 1 million copies in America alone, helping parent album *Come on Over* shift a staggering 36 million copies.

Twain wrote the song after critics claimed her relationship with music producer Lange was merely a ploy to further her career.

The song won several awards, including two Grammys (Best Country Song and Best Female Country Vocal Performance); Best Selling Country Single at the 1998 Billboard Music Awards; Single of the Year at the 1998 Canadian Country Music Awards; and Song of the Year at the 1999 BMI Country Songwriter Awards and Broadcast Music Incorporated (BMI) Pop Songwriter Awards.

The video was similarly lauded, winning Best Country Video Award at the 1998

Billboard Music Video Awards; Video of the Year at the 1998 CMT Latin America Awards; and the Viewer's Choice Award for Sexiest Video at the 1998 VH1 Viewer's Choice Awards. In 2006, the BMI announced 'You're Still The One' had been played over 6 million times on American radio.

Alanis Morissette 'You Oughta Know'

Alanis Morissette's anti-love album *Jagged Little Pill* was a huge critical and commercial smash, eventually selling 33 million copies.

The album's feisty sound was showcased on the hit single 'You Oughta Know', a furious rant against an ex-lover. With lyrics such as: "Does she speak eloquently, and would she have your baby? I'm sure she'd make a really excellent mother… and every time you speak her name, does she know how you told me you'd hold me until you died? But you're still alive," it was clear Alanis was not to be messed with.

She has never publicly acknowledged who the song is aimed at, but various rumours have suggested the actors Dave Coulier, Bob Saget or Matt LeBlanc, the hockey player Mike Peluso and the musician Leslie Howe.

Whitney Houston *The Bodyguard* (Soundtrack)

Despite mixed reviews, Kevin Costner and Whitney Houston's romantic thriller *The Bodyguard* enjoyed huge box office success in 1992, and went on to spawn the bestselling soundtrack of all time. The album, which featured six Whitney Houston tracks (including 'I Will Always Love You', see below) and six contributions from other artists, sold 42 million copies. It also holds the title of being the first record to sell over a million copies in one week, a feat it achieved in America six weeks after being released.

Whitney Houston 'I Will Always Love You'

Whitney's cover of Dolly Parton's 'I Will Always Love You' almost never happened – the singer was due to record Jimmy Ruffin's 'What Becomes of the Broken-hearted' for *The Bodyguard*, but changed her mind at the last minute after hearing the song was already being used for *Fried Green Tomatoes* at the Whistlestop Café. Houston's *Bodyguard* co-star Kevin Costner is said to have suggested Parton's track, and both insisted the song should keep its now-famous a cappella introduction, despite strong opposition from the record company. It's a good job the label listened to them – 'I Will Always Love You' became one of Houston's best-known songs, selling 12 million copies worldwide. It managed an enormous 14 weeks at the top in America, and 10 weeks at number 1 in Australia and the UK.

Bryan Adams 'Everything I Do (I Do It For You)'

Bryan Adams' 'Everything I Do (I Do It For You)' was inescapable in the UK in the summer of 1991 – its inclusion on the massively popular *Robin Hood: Prince of Thieves* soundtrack ensured the song stayed at number 1 for a mind-boggling 16 weeks. It also managed a comparatively normal seven weeks at the top in America, plus nine weeks in Canada. The slushy power ballad won the Grammy Award for Best Song Written Specifically for a Motion Picture or Television, and was also Oscar-nominated for Best Song.

Paula Abdul once sang: 'It ain't fiction, just a natural fact – we come together 'cause opposites attract.' This pair certainly agree…

The Lingo of Love

You never know when you might need to use it!

English	–	I love you
French	–	Je t'aime
Spanish	–	Te amo
Italian	–	Ti amo
German	–	Ich liebe dich
Swedish	–	Jag älskar dig ju
Welsh	–	Caru ti
Dutch	–	Ik hou van je
Chinese	–	Wo ie ni
Greek	–	S'ayapo
Japanese	–	Kimi o ai shiteru
Danish	–	Jeg elsker dig

Love never
goes out
of fashion

“Whatever our **souls** are made of **his** and **mine** are the **same**.”

Emily Brönte

Love songs

Jog your memory with more of the greatest love songs of all time…

Enrique Iglesias – 'Hero'

Enrique's 'Hero' took on a new significance in 2001 when the song became associated with firefighters, police and civilians involved in the devastating World Trade Center attacks.

Bill Medley and Jennifer Warnes – '(I've Had) The Time Of My Life'

The huge success of *Dirty Dancing* meant this song from its soundtrack charted twice in the UK – once in 1987 (number 6) and again in 1991 (number 8).

Elton John – 'Your Song'

'Your Song' was actually the B-side to Elton's 1970 single 'Take Me To The Pilot', but DJs opted to ignore the A-side – and the rest is history.

Shania Twain – 'You're Still The One'

Despite being one of her biggest songs, Shania's 1998 single 'You're Still The One' peaked at just number 2 on America's Billboard Hot 100. It did, however, reach the top in Canada.

Jackson Five – 'I'll Be There'

This song topped the US charts twice: once in 1970 and again in 1992 when Mariah Carey covered it.

Bonnie Tyler – 'Total Eclipse Of The Heart'

At the peak of its popularity, 'Total Eclipse' was estimated to be selling a staggering 60,000 copies a day.

Marvin Gaye – 'Let's Get It On'

'Let's Get It On' originally contained religious lyrics. Gaye changed his mind and redrafted them with a political edge before finally settling on the famous love imagery we are familiar with today.

Sinead O'Connor – 'Nothing Compares 2 U'

Prince and The Family's 'Nothing Compares 2 U' first appeared on the 1985 album *The Family*, but wasn't a hit until Sinead O'Connor's cover in 1990.

Bee Gees – 'How Deep Is Your Love'

'How Deep Is Your Love' first appeared on the *Saturday Night Fever* soundtrack in 1977. Take That released their version as a swansong in 1996, before re-forming in 2005

Madonna – 'Crazy For You'

Madonna's 'Crazy For You' first appeared on the *Vision Quest* soundtrack in 1985, and then on her 1990 compilation *The Immaculate Collection*. The song was also included on her 1995 ballads collection *Something to Remember*.

Love songs

Barry Manilow – 'Mandy'

In the well-known Simpsons episode 'The Last Temptations Of Homer', Homer Simpson alters the lyrics of 'Mandy' after wife Marge finds a turkey behind a hotel bed. His version goes: 'Oh Margey, you came and you found me a turkey, on my vacation away from work-y!'

Robbie Williams – 'Angels'

Robbie's 1997 smash 'Angels' has sold over 2 million copies and is widely credited as being the song that saved his floundering pop career.

Cyndi Lauper – 'Time After Time'

Lauper's second biggest single globally – just behind 'Girls Just Want To Have Fun.'

Eric Clapton – 'Wonderful Tonight'

'Wonderful Tonight' is taken from Clapton's 1977 album *Slowhand* and is a tribute to the model and photographer Pattie Boyd.

Sonny and Cher – 'I Got You Babe'

This classic hippie tune from 1965 was re-released in the UK in 1993 after being used repeatedly in the movie *Groundhog Day*.

George Michael – 'Careless Whisper'

1984's 'Careless Whisper' was George Michael's first solo single, though he was still performing with Wham! at the time. In America, the track was credited to Wham!, featuring George Michael.

Dolly Parton and Kenny Rogers – 'Islands In The Stream'

In 2005, Country Music Television voted Parton and Rogers' 1983 hit 'Islands In The Stream' the best country duet of all time.

Chris Isaak – 'Wicked Game'

'Wicked Game' was released in 1989 but didn't become a hit until 1991, when it was included on director David Lynch's *Wild at Heart* soundtrack.

Al Green – 'Let's Stay Together'

'Let's Stay Together' topped the charts in 1972 and was also a huge hit for Tina Turner in 1983.

Toni Braxton – 'Un-Break My Heart'

Toni Braxton's 'Un-Break My Heart' was a US number 1 for 11 weeks in a row in late 1996 and early 1997. It stalled at number 2 in the UK behind Dunblane charity record 'Knockin' On Heaven's Door', and later the Spice Girls with '2 Become 1'.

Celebrity Weddings

The phenomenon of celebrity weddings is nothing new, but they are no longer the sole preserve of high society figures, pop stars and A-list actors. With the increasing media exposure granted to reality stars and footballers, the celebrity wedding is becoming ever more commonplace – not to mention lavish to the point of outrage. But as the following examples prove, some celebrities clearly put more effort into their big day than the marriage that followed. From the impossibly glitzy to the downright trashy, here are some of the world's most notorious celebrity weddings:

Elizabeth Taylor and ....

Details of Elizabeth Taylor's marriages could probably fill a book of their own – the Hollywood legend has had no less than eight 'big days' with seven different men. Here is a list of her husbands – and the dates of their time with Taylor:

Conrad "Nicky" Hilton (6th May 1950–29th January 1951) (divorced); Michael Wilding (21st February 1952–26th January 1957) (divorced); Michael Todd (2nd February 1957–22nd March 1958) (widowed); Eddie Fisher (12th May 1959–6th March 1964) (divorced); Richard Burton (15th March 1964–26th June 1974) (divorced); Richard Burton (again) (10th October 1975–29th July 1976) (divorced); John Warner (4th December 1976–7th November 1982) (divorced); Larry Fortensky (6th October 1991–31st October 1996) (divorced).

That's a lot of wedding presents!

Jackie and John F Kennedy

As a noted fashionista and wife to the 35th US President, it comes as little surprise that Jackie's 1953 wedding dress is the most-photographed in history. The wedding guests alone must have contributed to a high number of these pictures – over 700 attended, while 900 gathered at the reception afterwards. Despite the promising start, they briefly separated for a number of personal problems, but eventually reconciled. The couple produced four children, but their first, a daughter, was stillborn. The fourth, Patrick, died after just two days. To add to the tragedy, Kennedy was assassinated in 1963.

Catherine Zeta Jones and Michael Douglas

The 25-year age gap between actors Catherine Zeta Jones and Michael Douglas wasn't the only controversy of their 2000 wedding – leaked photographs from the big day resulted in a multi-million pound lawsuit which took years to settle.

The Douglases had pre-agreed to a £1 million exclusivity deal allowing *OK!* magazine to cover their nuptials, but rival magazine *Hello!* successfully obtained and published photos of the event before *OK!*'s commemorative issue was released. *OK!* and the Douglases immediately sued *Hello!*, leading to much legal to-ing and fro-ing. *OK!* was initially awarded £1 million in damages, but was later ordered to repay the money after a successful appeal by *Hello!*. In 2007, the House of Lords made a partial ruling in favour of *OK!*; the case was revealed to have cost £8 million at that point.

The Douglases received a paltry £14,600 in damages during the original 2003 hearing – a figure far outweighed by the negative publicity surrounding the case.

David Beckham and Victoria Adams

The pairing of "Posh" Spice Girl Victoria Adams with footballer David Beckham was a match made in tabloid heaven. They were young, beautiful, rich – and rarely seen without coordinating outfits, jewellery and tattoos. Back then, Victoria was easily the more famous of the two, but their marriage and subsequent launch of "Brand Beckham" sent both of their profiles into the stratosphere. Their 1999 wedding was major news – unsurprising, given the enormous tabloid interest in their 1998 engagement.

The big day was expected to be over-the-top, and the flashy couple did not disappoint: customized, elevated thrones for the bride and groom (with space for baby Brooklyn's crib at their side); matching designer wedding outfits in cream (with a swift costume change before the reception); an 18-piece orchestra; fireworks; and a black-and-white dress code for guests. The whole event was covered exclusively by *OK!* magazine in a precedent-setting £1 million deal, resulting in *OK!*'s third-highest selling issue.

The couple went on to have two more boys, Romeo and Cruz, and are still going strong a decade later.

NY

Madonna and Sean Penn (and Guy Ritchie)

One of Madonna's most outrageous moments was marrying bad-boy actor Sean Penn in 1985. Their short-lived and volatile marriage didn't get off to a promising start; on their wedding day, Penn is said to have fired a gun at a press helicopter circling overhead. The pair divorced in 1989, but not before Penn was charged with felony domestic assault.

The Material Girl gave marriage another shot in 2000, exchanging vows with film director Guy Ritchie in a heavily guarded, £1.5 million ceremony at Scotland's Skibo Castle.

Despite bringing up three children and playing happy families for almost a decade, they eventually announced their divorce in 2008. The settlement saw Ritchie walking away with just a country house... rumoured to be worth tens of millions of pounds. Not a bad little bachelor pad, really.

Paul McCartney and Heather Mills

Former Beatle Paul McCartney surprised fans in 2002 by marrying outspoken model Heather Mills – just three years after the death of his beloved first wife, Linda.

Mills and McCartney married in a £3 million ceremony at Ireland's Castle Leslie in front of a star-studded audience including Ringo Starr, Eric Clapton, Sir Elton John, the Pretenders' Chrissie Hynde, Pink Floyd's Dave Gilmour and tennis champion Monica Seles. Baby Beatrice soon followed, but in 2008 McCartney was handing over cash and assets worth £24 million in a bid to get Mills out of his life.

Katie Price and Peter Andre

British viewers were glued to their screens when glamour model Katie Price – a.k.a. Jordan – appeared on ITV's hit reality show *I'm A Celebrity… Get Me Out Of Here!* It wasn't long before romance blossomed between Price and fellow contestant, Aussie heartthrob and former pop star Peter Andre.

Despite suggestions that their onscreen chemistry was fake, the pair stayed together after filming, eventually marrying in late 2005. Price arrived at the ceremony in a Cinderella-style horse-drawn carriage, and wore a gigantic pink puffball dress. Her bridesmaids were Girls Aloud's Sarah Harding, Liberty X's Michelle Heaton and former Atomic Kitten Kerry Katona.

Price and Andre went on to make a fortune by allowing TV cameras into their home for a series of post-wedding reality shows, but divorced in 2009.

Chris Evans and Billie Piper

Zany TV and radio personality-turned-media mogul Chris Evans raised eyebrows in 2001 when he wed teen pop star Billie Piper. The unlikely pair – he was 35 and she was 18 – announced their engagement after a whirlwind six-month relationship, but scrapped their original wedding plans for a "quickie" Vegas bash. The £200 ceremony took place four months earlier than expected, but the marriage fizzled out three years later. Although their separation was announced in 2005, the divorce was not finalized until 2007. Both have since remarried and remain on good terms.

Britney Spears and Kevin Federline (and Jason Alexander)

Britney kept busy in 2004 with not one but two marriages – one in January and one in September.

The first was to childhood friend Jason Alexander, and appeared to be the result of a particularly wild night out in Vegas. Unsurprisingly, the marriage was annulled just 55 hours later – but six months passed and a presumably bored Britney announced another engagement, this time to boyfriend-of-three-months, dancer Kevin Federline.

They married in a surprise wedding in California with just 20 guests, and although Spears and K-Fed had two boys, Sean Preston and Jayden James, they divorced two years later.

A Cocktail for Lovers

Ingredients:

Handful of ice
½ oz/15 ml Amaretto
½ oz/15 ml Cherry Brandy
½ oz/15 ml Crème de Cacao
1 oz/30 ml cream
½ oz/15 ml whipping cream

Method:

Shake the Amaretto, Cherry Brandy, Crème de Cacao and cream in a cocktail shaker filled with ice.
Strain into a chilled Martini glass.
Top with whipped cream.

Sonnet from the Portuguese XLIII

"How do I love thee? Let me count the ways.
I love thee to the depth and breadth and height
My soul can reach, when feeling out of sight
For the ends of Being and ideal Grace.
I love thee to the level of everyday's
Most quiet need, by sun and candlelight.
I love thee freely, as men strive for Right;
I love thee with the passion put to use
In my old griefs, and with my childhood's faith.
I love thee with a love I seemed to lose
With my lost saints, – I love thee with the breath,
Smiles, tears, of all my life! – and, if God choose,
I shall but love thee better after death."

Elizabeth Barrett Browning

Love songs

Found your favourite classic yet?

Extreme – 'More Than Words'

Although Extreme found fame in the UK before their homeland of America, their 1991 single 'More Than Words' peaked at number 2 in the UK and reached number 1 in the US.

Commodores – 'Three Times A Lady'

This famous 1978 ballad was said to have been inspired by composer Lionel Richie's three leading ladies: his wife, his mother and his grandmother.

Leann Rimes – 'How Do I Live'

Although Rimes' 1997 hit 'How Do I Live' peaked at number 7 in the UK, it remained on the chart for a whopping 34 weeks.

Peter Frampton – 'Baby, I Love Your Way'

Although a big hit for Frampton in 1975, Big Mountain's reggae cover from 1994 is arguably the most enduring version.

Boyz II Men – 'I'll Make Love To You'

Boyz II Men's slushy 1994 ballad reached number 5 in the UK, but stayed at number 1 in America for 14 weeks!

Roberta Flack – 'First Time Ever I Saw Your Face'

Flack's 1969 cover of Ewan MacColl's 1957 folk song gained enormous popularity after being used in Clint Eastwood's directorial debut *Play Misty For Me*.

Stevie Wonder – 'I Just Called To Say I Love You'

Although critics were disappointed by Wonder's simplistic pop track 'I Just Called To Say I Love You', it went on to become one of his biggest hits.

Pretenders – 'I'll Stand By You'

A major hit in its own right for the Pretenders in 1994, 'I'll Stand By You' went on to reach the top a decade later when it was covered by Girls Aloud.

Boston – 'More Than A Feeling'

Boston's wistful rock song 'More Than A Feeling' is said to have influenced Nirvana's breakout hit 'Smells Like Teen Spirit.'

Vanessa Williams – 'Save The Best For Last'

This 1991 ballad has two videos – the second, featuring romantic winter scenes, ensured the song re-charted over several Christmas holidays.

Top Romantic Destinations

Maldives

With over 200 inhabited islands, there's no shortage of secluded beaches to choose from in the Maldives. Little surprise, then, that it has become a hot favourite with loved-up couples.

Thailand

Known for its welcoming faces and impeccable hospitality, Thailand is full of spectacular and romantic settings. From Bangkok's hustle and bustle to the tranquillity of its many island beaches (where you will find tiny huts for two), there's something for all in the land of smiles.

Italy

Its language is synonymous with love, so no wonder honeymooners flock to Italian cities such as Venice, Florence and Rome. If you're visiting and feel you've absorbed enough culture, why not take your loved one to the spectacular Amalfi coast?

Paris

The iconic backdrop of Paris will forever be linked with romance – the views from the Eiffel Tower, the gothic splendour of Notre Dame Cathedral, the Arc de Triomphe, lovers kissing on the bridges of the river Seine, the beautiful food and sexy, chic people... it just has that certain *je ne sais quoi*.

New York

Kissing in Times Square, strolling through Central Park, proposing atop the Empire State Building?

Prague

Prague's enchanting and romantic buildings have led to the nickname 'The city of 100 spires' – just make sure the awe-inspiring architecture doesn't cause you to forget your partner!

St Lucia

St Lucia's tropical scenery and dramatic mountain peaks form the backdrop to a host of heavenly beaches. Oprah Winfrey called it one of the top five places to visit in your lifetime – so make sure you go with somebody special.

Niagara Falls

For over 200 years, honeymooning couples have visited Niagara Falls to absorb the mesmerizing landscape and jaw-dropping waterfalls. Be warned – if you propose there, your partner may not hear you over the crashing water!

Hawaii

Azure waters, swaying palms, matching his-n-hers *leis* – who wouldn't like to get married with an authentic Hawaiian flower garland around their neck?

Fiji

With turquoise sea, powder soft sands and glorious sunshine – and hammocks on the beach for two. Book those plane tickets now!

I LOVE
YOU!

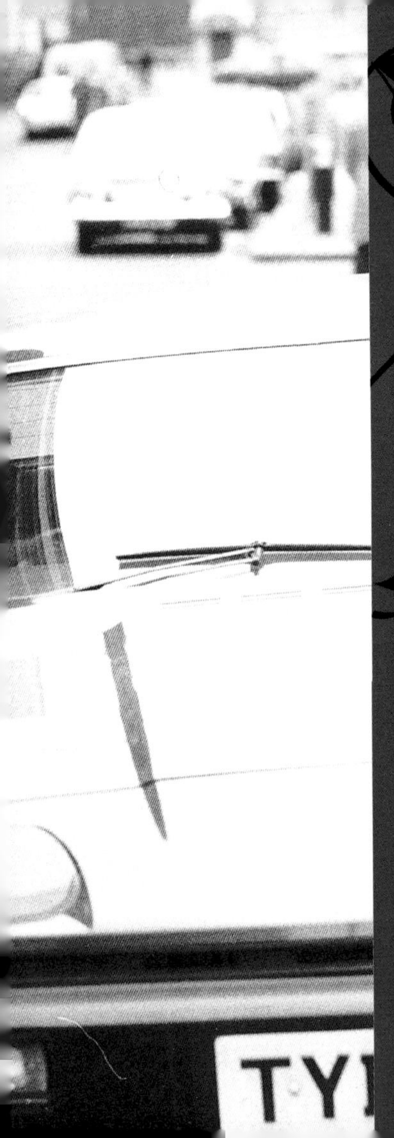

Well, it was worth a try...

Monuments to Love

Many famous buildings were created to honour a loved one – here are some facts and figures about these love landmarks.

Taj Mahal

The Taj Mahal was built by Mughal Emperor Shah Jahan in memory of his favourite wife, Mumtaz Mahal, who died during the birth of their 14th child. It is said that her dying wish was for Shah Jahan to build her the finest mausoleum the world had ever known.

The stunning marble structure was constructed between 1632 and 1652, and is considered the finest example of Mughal architecture, a style with Persian, Indian and Islamic influences. Located in Agra, India, the Taj Mahal is a UNESCO World Heritage Site and receives between 2 and 4 million visitors a year.

Hanging Gardens of Babylon

The Hanging Gardens of Babylon are said to have been one of the original Seven Wonders of the World, and were located near present-day Al Hillah, Babil, Iraq.

King Nebuchadnezzar II built the gardens around 600 BCE as a gesture of sympathy towards his sick wife, Amytis of Media, who reportedly missed the flora and fauna of her native Persia. Sadly, the gardens no longer remain, thanks to a series of earthquakes after the second century BCE – though some have claimed they never actually existed and were merely a poetic creation.

The Royal Pavilion, Brighton

Although Brighton's striking Royal Pavilion was not "built out of love", it was certainly used for it. The Pavilion came into being in 1786, when the Prince Regent – who had been enjoying the medicinal qualities of Brighton's sea since 1783 – rented a farmhouse in the Old Steine area. The bolt-hole provided a private meeting place in which the amorous Prince was able to court his lover, Mrs Fitzherbert, whom he was unable to marry on account of her Catholicism.

The Prince soon purchased additional land surrounding the property, adding a riding school and stables built in an Indian style. The architect John Nash redesigned the Pavilion between 1815 and 1822, giving it the distinctive look we see today.

The Eleanor Crosses

The Eleanor Crosses were a series of 12 crosses built by Edward I between 1291 and 1294 in honour of his late wife, Eleanor of Castile. Only three of the impressive stone monuments remain, and these can be found at Waltham Cross and Geddington town centres, as well as Northampton's Delapré Abbey.

The original 12 were built in a line down part of the east of England, and were located (in order) at: Lincoln, Grantham, Stamford, Geddington, Hardingstone (Northampton), Stony Stratford, Woburn, Dunstable, St Albans, Waltham (now Waltham Cross), Westcheap (now Cheapside) and Charing Cross.

BLOCK
POINT

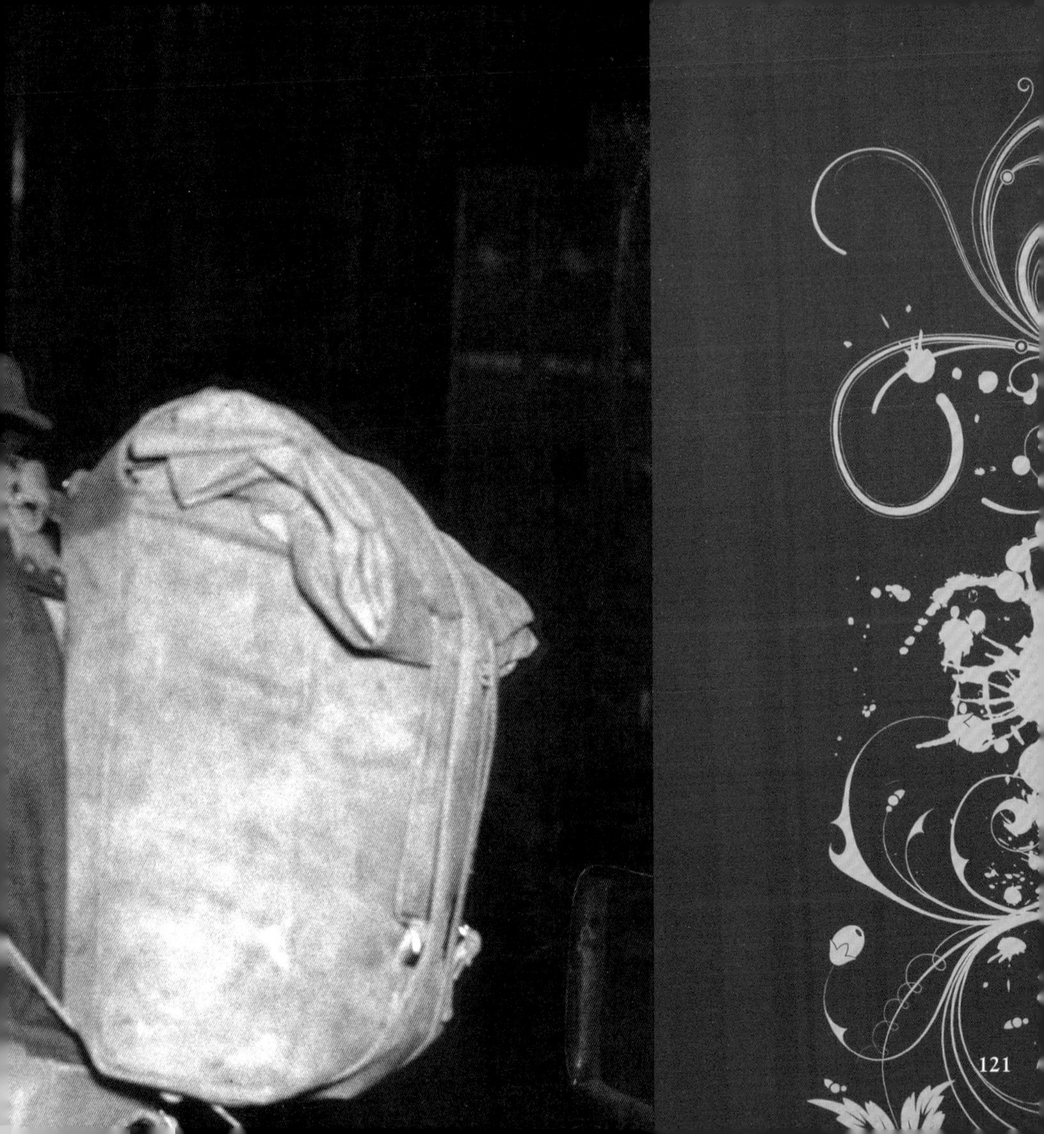

Kissing facts

- In humans, 34 facial muscles and 112 postural muscles are used during a kiss.

- The orbicularis oris muscle is known as "the kissing muscle" as it is responsible for the puckering of the lips.

- Lips are packed with nerve endings so are sensitive to touch and bite.

- The deep kiss, or French kiss, is considered the art of making two mouths into one whole. In 2002, Madonna, Britney Spears and Christina Aguilera caused a sensation by French kissing while performing at the 20th annual MTV Video Music Awards. It is unclear how the French kiss got its name, but some believe it is because Paris is known as the city of love. Either way, the French do not call it French kissing!

- Kissing has several health benefits. It reduces stress, increases relationship satisfaction and is even said to lower cholesterol levels. So get snogging!

- It is not known if kissing is learned or instinctive. One theory posits that kissing could be related to grooming, while another suggests it came from mothers chewing their food before passing it to their offspring. How romantic…

Kissing facts

- Pheromones are passed through kissing, allowing us to assess the compatibility of potential mates.
- Non-human primates (such as lemurs, monkeys, and apes) are known to kiss.
- Rodin's famous marble sculpture *The Kiss* caused controversy in 1914 when it was placed on display in Lewes Town Hall. Certain prudish locals feared the erotic nature of the piece would "arouse" soldiers billeted in the town, and successfully campaigned to have it covered with a sheet. In 1955, the Tate Gallery of London purchased *The Kiss* for the princely sum of £7,500.

- If someone offers you a Glasgow kiss, we strongly advise running away!

- An Eskimo kiss – or a *Kunik*– involves pressing the nose and upper lip against the cheeks or forehead of a loved one and breathing in, causing their skin to be sucked against the nose and upper lip. In the West, this greeting has evolved into the marginally less intrusive act of rubbing noses together.

- In the Bible, Judas betrays Jesus with a kiss, an action which informed Roman soldiers of the whereabouts of their target.

Love songs

The last in our list of the biggest love songs of all time – which one holds special memories for you?

Chicago – 'If You Leave Me Now'

Chicago's unmistakeable ballad was number 1 on both sides of the pond in 1976.

Nat King Cole – 'Unforgettable'

This song was originally published in 1951, and was later remixed and released as a duet with Cole's daughter Natalie in 1992. This version went on to win three gongs at the 1992 Grammy Awards.

Mr Big – 'To Be With You'

Irish boyband Westlife covered Mr Big's biggest hit in 2003 during an acoustic section of their tour.

Heart – 'Alone'

'Alone' was a hit for power balladeers Heart in 1987, and was covered by Céline Dion 20 years later.

Air Supply – 'All Out Of Love'

Artists who have covered this song include Westlife (with Delta Goodrem), Jagged Edge, Enigma, John Barrowman and Cliff Richard!

Paul McCartney – 'Maybe I'm Amazed'

This 1970 song was written as an ode to Paul's wife Linda, who helped him during the aftermath of the Beatles' acrimonious split.

Dido – 'Thank You'

Although 'Thank You' featured in the 1998 movie *Sliding Doors*, it wasn't a hit until it appeared on Dido's 2001 album *No Angel*.

Barry White – 'You're The First, The Last, My Everything'

Godfather of Love Barry White's 'You're The First, The Last, My Everything' peaked at number 2 on the Billboard Hot 100 in 1974, but made it to the top for two weeks in the UK.

Foreigner – 'I Want To Know What Love Is'

1984's 'I Want To Know What Love Is' remains a big radio hit, charting in the Top 25 most played songs on American radio in 2000, 2001 and 2002.

Alicia Keys – 'Fallin''

Keys' 2001 debut single 'Fallin'' is her second biggest hit after 2007's 'No One'.

> “My bounty is as boundless as the sea,
> My love as deep; the more I give to thee,
> The more I have, for both are infinite.”

William Shakespeare
Romeo and Juliet

William Shakespeare – not just the most famous English writer of all time, but arguably the greatest. His texts have been translated into almost all living languages, and, centuries after his death, remain the most studied and performed work of any playwright.

His poems, sonnets and plays deal with love in all its forms – comedic, tragic, passionate and romantic – and feature countless memorable quotes. Who could forget these famous lines of love?

"O Romeo, Romeo! Wherefore art thou Romeo?"

Romeo and Juliet

"If music be the food of love, play on."

Twelfth Night

"The course of true love never did run smooth."

A Midsummer Night's Dream

"I know no ways to mince it in love, but directly to say 'I love you'."

Henry V1

"She's beautiful, and therefore to be wooed;
She is woman, and therefore to be won."

Henry VI

"I would not wish any companion
in the world but you."

The Tempest

"Doubt thou the stars are fire, doubt the sun doth
move, doubt truth to be a liar, but never doubt
thy love."

Hamlet

"I humbly do beseech of your pardon,
for too much loving you."

Othello

"The sight of lovers feedeth
those in love."

As You Like It

More ways to say I love you...

- Tell them how great they look.
- Without complaining, allow them to go shopping / watch sport (delete as appropriate!).
- Never forget the importance of hugs and kisses.
- On a winter's morning, sneak out and warm their car up for them. Don't leave the keys in the ignition, though – a stolen car would slightly spoil the gesture.
- Spell out "I love you" using their favourite sweets.

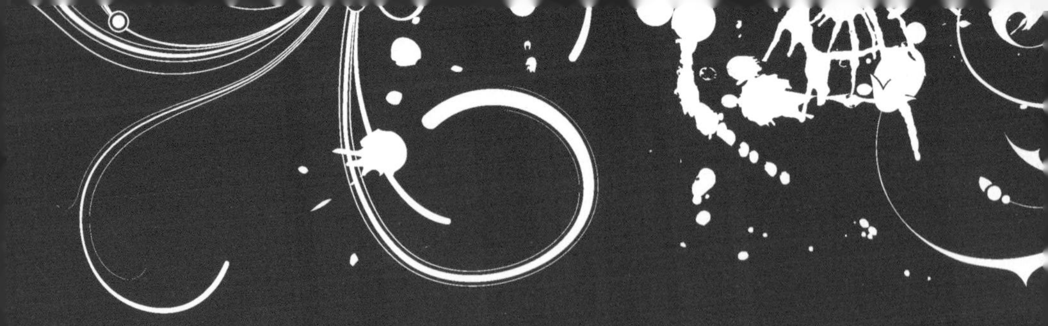

- Prepare a special dinner – or simply make their favourite dish. Don't forget the candles!
- This one requires considerable skill, not to mention a large garden – using a lawn mower, cut "I love you" into the grass.
- Hide a love note in a book they are reading, or… turn their screensaver into a love note.
- Whisk them away for a surprise day out devoted to their enjoyment.

Good luck – and don't be afraid to try out your own ideas!

“If you **wish** to be **loved, love**.”

Lucius Seneca

Love Quiz 2

1. What year was Richard Curtis' Love Actually released?
2. Who released an album entitled Lovesexy in 1988?
3. Who said, "Today is a magnificent day for me, I'm engaged to a magnificent woman," and who were they talking about?
4. How long were Pamela Anderson and Kid Rock married for?
5. Which singer not only felt love, but also "loved to love you baby"?
6. 'Il Creatore' bridal wear in Hungary is said to have set the world record for longest wedding-dress train – but how long was it?
7. What do Bob Geldof, Britney Spears, Joan Collins and Bruce Willis all have in common?
8. What are Shannon Sickles and Grainne Close known for?
9. At the peak of its popularity, how many copies of Bonnie Tyler's 'Total Eclipse Of The Heart' were said to have sold per day?
10. Which film contains the line "Hearts will be practical only when they are made unbreakable"?

Answers on page 175

make love not war

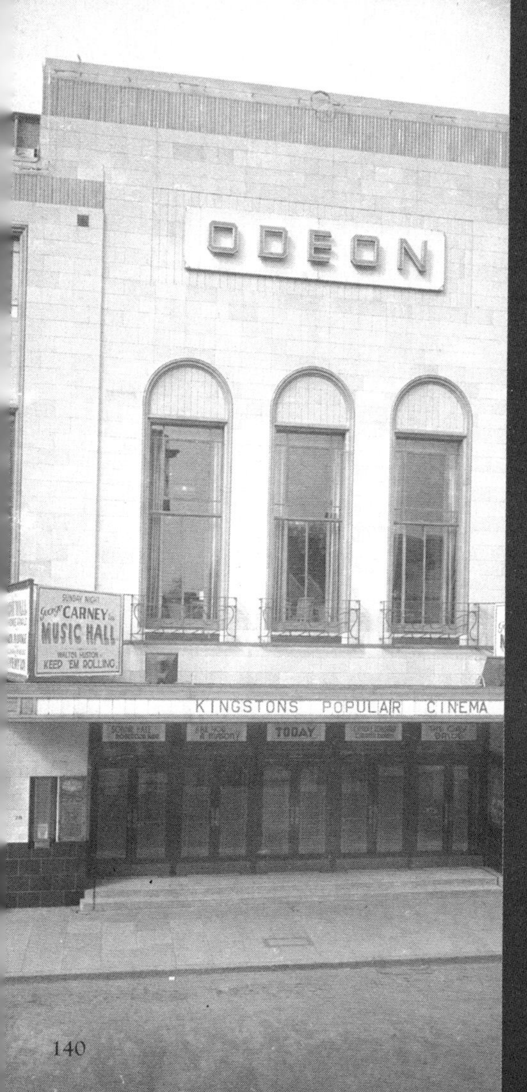

Love on Film

The history of cinema is rich with memorable love scenes. Who could forget a naval-suited Richard Gere lifting Debra Winger at the close of *An Officer And A Gentleman*, or *Crocodile Dundee's* Paul Hogan being helped across a packed subway platform in order to reach Linda Kozlowski?

Who didn't shed a tear as icy waters separated Leonardo DiCaprio and Kate Winslet in *Titanic*, or cheer as a rain-sodden Hugh Grant finally agreed "not" to marry Andie MacDowell in *Four Weddings and a Funeral*?

Although these scenes are easily pictured in the mind, the real reason they endure is not simply the romantic visuals, but the winning combination of beautiful imagery with classic dialogue.

With this in mind, here is a collection of moving quotes from cinema's biggest love stories. Which one makes you shed a tear?

Casablanca

"Of all the gin joints in all the towns in all the world, she walks into mine."

Notting Hill

"Don't forget. I'm just a girl standing in front of a boy... asking him to love her."

Good Will Hunting

"It doesn't matter if the guy is perfect or the girl is perfect, as long as they are perfect for each other."

Moulin Rouge

"The greatest thing you'll ever learn is just to love and be loved in return."

Love Actually

"Tell her that you love her. You've got nothing to lose, and you'll always regret it if you don't."

Twilight

"I dream about being with you forever."

Four Weddings and a Funeral

"The truth is... well, the truth is, I have met the right person, and he's not in love with me, and until I stop loving him, no one else really has a chance."

City of Angels

"I would rather have had one breath of her hair, one kiss from her mouth, one touch of her hand, than eternity without it."

When Harry Met Sally

"I came here tonight because when you realize you want to spend the rest of your life with somebody, you want the rest of your life to start as soon as possible."

Crouching Tiger Hidden Dragon

"I would rather be a ghost, drifting by your side, as a condemned soul, than enter heaven without you. Because of your love, I will never be a lonely spirit."

Great Expectations

"She'll only break your heart, it's a fact. And even though I warn you, even though I guarantee you that the girl will only hurt you terribly, you'll still pursue her. Ain't love grand?"

Gone With The Wind

"I've loved you more than I've ever loved any woman and I've waited for you longer than I've ever waited for any woman."

Titanic

"Promise me you'll survive. That you won't give up, no matter what happens, no matter how hopeless. Promise me now, Rose, and never let go of that promise."

It's A Wonderful Life

"What is it you want, Mary? What do you want? You want the moon? Just say the word and I'll throw a lasso around it and pull it down. Hey. That's a pretty good idea. I'll give you the moon, Mary."

"You had me at hello."

Little Women

"I've loved you from the moment I first laid eyes on you. What would be more reasonable than to marry you?"

The Wizard of Oz

"Hearts will be practical only when they are made unbreakable."

Pet names for loved ones...

Most people keep their pet names a secret, and with good reason. Here are some of the most popular - is yours in there?

Special
Treasure
Buttercup
Gorgeous
Handsome
Kitten
Hunk
Sweetheart
Tiger
Honey
Darling
Queenie
Big Boy
Snowy
Princess
Loverboy
Cowboy
Cheeky
Puppy Stud
Bambi
Burrito
Kitty
Snuggles
Squashy
Hot Lips
Monkey
Boo
Schmoo

Motherly love

Never underestimate the power of your mother's love – it may have changed your genetic code.

Although our individual "biological blueprint" is said to be in place before birth, scientists observing animals have discovered that offspring receiving greater levels of maternal care grow up to be less fearful and more adventurous. From this, they have theorized that motherly affection may be responsible for altering the gene that controls the brain's response to stress.

If true, this theory implies that we humans can adapt to our surroundings far more quickly than previously thought – millions of years more quickly…

And remember: Fatherly love is 'Never Gonna Give You Up' either!

I'M
RICK
ASTLEY'S
DAD
WELL DONE
RICK ASTLEY
YOU'VE ALWAYS BEEN
OUR Nº1 LOVE YOU

A Birthday

My heart is like a singing bird
Whose nest is in a watered shoot;
My heart is like an apple-tree
Whose boughs are bent with thick-set fruit;
My heart is like a rainbow shell
That paddles in a halcyon sea;
My heart is gladder than all these,
Because my love is come to me.

Raise me a dais of silk and down;
Hang it with vair and purple dyes;
Carve it in doves and pomegranates
And peacocks with a hundred eyes;
Work it in gold and silver grapes,
In leaves and silver fleurs-de-lys;
Because the birthday of my life
Is come, my love is come to me.

Christina G. Rossetti

Great Television Couples

Our favourite sitcoms, dramas and soap operas would be lost without the chemistry of their most popular couples.

From the happily married to the falling apart, the on again/off again to the will they/won't they? – all have kept us gripped. Here are some of television's most enduring partnerships and a recap of their colourful histories.

EastEnders: Angie and Den Watts

The Queen Vic has played host to many warring couples, but Den and Angie Watts were the soap's ultimate volatile pairing. When landlord Dennis "Dirty Den" Watts (Leslie Grantham) surprised alcoholic Angie (Anita Dobson) with divorce papers on Christmas Day, a record-breaking 30 million viewers tuned in to watch the collapse of their 20-year marriage.

Coronation Street: Jack and Vera Duckworth

The turbulent marriage of Jack (Bill Tarmey) and Vera's (Elizabeth Dawn), arguably *Coronation Street's* best-loved couple, survived infidelity, the strife brought on by wayward son Terry – not least the revelation that he wasn't Jack's son after all – and a second wedding in Vegas after Jack revealed he had lied about his age at the original ceremony, rendering it invalid. When Vera eventually passed away, viewers mourned her no-nonsense wit and famous catchphrase, "Don't you love me anymore, Jack?"

Sex and the City: Carrie and Mr Big

Sex and the City lead Carrie Bradshaw (Sarah Jessica Parker) is an expert on sex, shoes and shopping – but can't seem to apply these skills to her personal life. Despite a number of semi-promising relationships (remember hunky Aidan, insecure Berger and patronizing Aleksandr?), Carrie's heart has always belonged to Mr Big (Chris Noth) – and boy, does she like telling us about it!

Big appeared in the very first episode of *Sex and the City*, and his subsequent "on-off" relationship with Carrie was drawn out for the show's entire run, eventually spilling over into the hugely popular spin-off movie. After several break-ups and Big's betrothal to another (during which he sleeps with Carrie, naturally), the turbulent pair finally marry – but not before Big jilts her at the altar one last time, of course.

Neighbours: Scott and Charlene

Australian soap *Neighbours* found its own Romeo and Juliet (almost) with the introduction of teen pin-ups Scott (Jason Donovan) and Charlene (Kylie Minogue). Despite opposition from their warring families, nothing could keep the young lovers apart, and their 1987 wedding was a huge ratings draw in both Australia and the UK. Angry Anderson's rock-ballad 'Suddenly', which soundtracked the couple's wedding, went on to top the Australian charts as well as reaching number 3 in the UK.

We hear Kylie and Jason did rather well out of the whole thing as well…

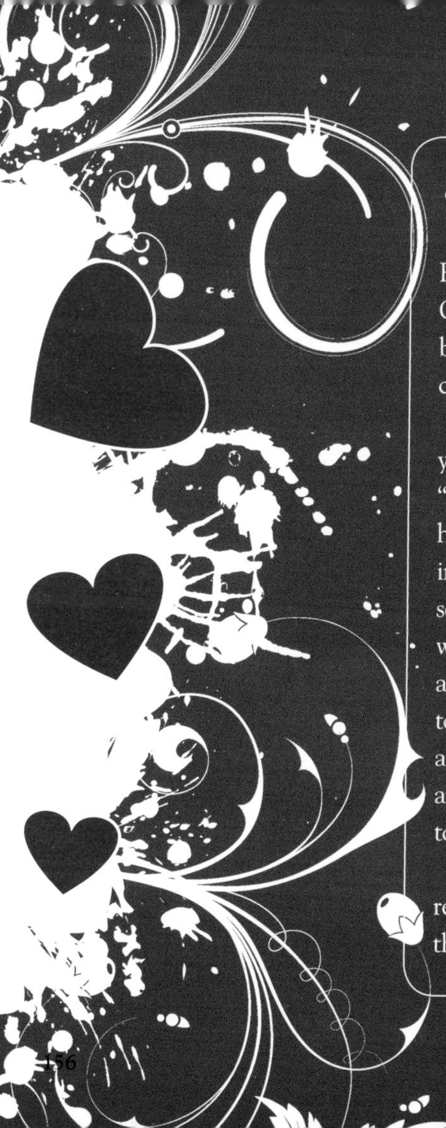

Friends: Ross and Rachel

Ross Geller (David Schwimmer) and Rachel Green (Jennifer Aniston) remain one of the best-loved – and occasionally infuriating – couples in comedy.

They endured countless ups and downs in the 10-year history of *Friends*, such as a comically protracted "will they/won't they" courtship – dating back to high school, on Ross' part; a disastrous "break" in which Ross "cheated" on Rachel; an uneasy separation in which they took turns to be jealous while pretending to be fine about their new life apart; Ross saying Rachel's name during his wedding to British girlfriend Emily; a drunken Vegas wedding; an unplanned baby; Rachel's new job in Paris… and don't even get us started on the time Rachel got together with Joey!

In case you missed the final episode, we won't reveal the conclusion… but, honestly, what do you think happened?

Cheers: Sam and Diane

The relationship between streetwise bartender Sam Malone (Ted Danson) and naïve, fish-out-of-water barmaid Diane Chambers (Shelley Long) was a staple of popular American sitcom *Cheers* for the first five seasons, and provided the template for countless "will they/won't they" sitcom couples.

The mismatched pair had little in common other than a mutual sexual attraction, but this did not deter Sam from proposing to Diane several times – and being rejected in a variety of comical ways. The show grew in popularity when Sam and Diane were officially together, and when Long left *Cheers* for good, Sam was immediately given another unlikely partner to spar relentlessly with – the feisty Rebecca Howe (Kirstie Alley).

Those were just a few examples of memorable on screen partnerships – remember these?

- *Buffy the Vampire Slayer* – Buffy and Angel (Sarah Michelle Gellar and David Boreanaz)
- *Dawson's Creek* – Dawson and Joey / Pacey and Joey (James Van Der Beek and Katie Holmes / Joshua Jackson and Katie Holmes)
- *Desperate Housewives* – Lynette and Tom Scarvo (Felicity Huffman and Doug Savant) / Susan Mayer and Mike Delfino (Teri Hatcher and James Denton) / Gabrielle and Carlos Solis (Eva Longoria Parker and Ricardo Chavira) / Bree and Orson Hodge (Marcia Cross and Kyle MacLachlan)
- *Doctor Who* – The Doctor and Rose (David Tennant and Billie Piper)
- *E.R.* – Dr. Doug Ross and Nurse Carol Hathaway (George Clooney and Julianna Margulies)
- *Fawlty Towers* – Basil and Sybil (John Cleese and Prunella Scales)
- *Frasier* – Niles and Daphne (David Hyde Pierce and Jane Leeves)
- *Futurama* – Fry and Leela (Billy West and Katey Sagal)
- *Gavin & Stacey* – Gavin and Stacey / Smithy and Nessa (Mathew Horne and Joanna Page / James Corden and Ruth Jones)
- *George and Mildred* – (Brian Murphy and Yootha Joyce)

- *Married with Children* – Al and Peggy Bundy (Ed O'Neill and Katey Sagal)
- *Moonlighting* – Madelyn 'Maddie' Hayes and David Addison Jr (Bruce Willis and Cybil Shepherd)
- *Mork and Mindy* – (Robin Williams and Pam Dawber)
- *The New Adventures of Superman* – Clark Kent and Lois Lane (Dean Cain and Teri Hatcher)
- *Roseanne* – Roseanne and Dan Connor (Roseanne Barr and John Goodman)
- *The Royle Family* – Dave and Denise (Craig Cash and Caroline Aherne)
- *Scrubs* – JD & Elliot (Zach Braff & Sarah Chalke)
- *The Sopranos* – Tony and Carmela Soprano (James Gandolfini and Edie Falco)
- *Terry and June* – (Terry Scott and June Whitfield)
- *This Life* – Egg and Milly / Anna and Miles (Andrew Lincoln and Amita Dhiri / Daniela Nardini and Jack Davenport)
- *Will & Grace* – Will and Grace / Jack and Karen (Eric McCormack and Debra Messing / Sean Hayes and Megan Mullally)
- *The Wonder Years* – Kevin Arnold and Winnie Cooper (Fred Savage and Danica McKellar)
- *The X-Files* – Mulder and Scully (David Duchovny and Gillian Anderson)

Love letters

Although electronic means of communication have rather eclipsed the traditional, physical letter, our fondness for love notes has not subsided. Although nowadays a saucy text is more likely to be sent than an outpouring of emotion across reams of paper, this only adds to the novelty of receiving a bona fide love letter in the mail – so why not give it a go?

And remember: if you use the post, you are far less likely to accidentally send your missive to the wrong person!

Read this moving note from Winston Churchill to his wife Clementine and see if it inspires you:

My darling Clemmie,
In your letter from Madras you wrote some words very dear to me, about my having enriched your life. I cannot tell you what pleasure this gave me, because I always feel so overwhelmingly in your debt, if there can be accounts in love... What it has been to me to live all these years in your heart and companionship no phrases can convey.
Winston Churchill
(23rd January, 1935)

Love songs to have sold over a million copies in the UK:

- The Beatles 'She Loves You', 'I Wanna Hold Your Hand', 'Can't Buy Me Love', 'I Feel Fine' and 'We Can Work It Out'
- Brotherhood of Man 'Save Your Kisses For Me'
- John Travolta and Olivia Newton-John 'You're The One That I Want'
- Soft Cell 'Tainted Love'
- George Michael 'Careless Whisper'
- Stevie Wonder 'I Just Called To Say I Love You'
- Wham! 'Last Christmas'
- Jennifer Rush 'The Power Of Love'
- Bryan Adams 'Everything I Do (I Do It For You)'
- Whitney Houston 'I Will Always Love You'
- Wet Wet Wet 'Love Is All Around'
- Robson & Jerome 'Unchained Melody'
- Spice Girls '2 Become 1'

- Fugees 'Killing Me Softly'
- Various Artists 'Perfect Day'
- All Saints 'Never Ever'
- Céline Dion 'My Heart Will Go On'
- Boyzone 'No Matter What'
- Cher 'Believe'
- Kylie 'Can't Get You Out Of My Head'
- Gareth Gates 'Unchained Melody'

Famous love songs to have sold over a million copies yet *failed* to reach number 1 include Wham!'s 'Last Christmas' and Robbie Williams' 'Angels'.

Artists who reached number 1 with love songs but didn't have any more top 20 hits include: Ricky Valance 'Tell Laura I Love Her' (1960); Jane Birkin and Serge Gainsbourg 'Je T'aime...Moi Non Plus' (1969); and Steve Brookstein 'Against All Odds' (2005).

Royal Weddings

Queen Elizabeth II and Prince Philip

Princess Elizabeth II married Lieutenant Philip Mountbatten on 20th November 1947. Philip was previously known as Philippos of Greece and Denmark, though he renounced these titles shortly before the wedding, adopting his maternal grandparents' surname of Mountbatten. After the marriage he became known as the Duke of Edinburgh and later Prince Philip.

The union raised a few eyebrows – most notably for the fact that Philip had no financial standing, plus the fact his sisters had Nazi links through marriage. In post-war Britain, this ensured they were barred from the wedding.

Despite these controversies, the happy couple successfully wed and were said to have received up to 2,500 presents from around the world.

The couple have since welcomed four children into the world: Charles, Prince of Wales; Anne, Princess Royal; Prince Andrew, Duke of York; and Prince Edward, Earl of Wessex.

Queen Elizabeth – who succeeded to the throne in 1952 – is one of Britain's longest reigning monarchs, while Prince Philip has become Britain's longest-serving consort and the oldest serving partner of a reigning monarch.

Grace Kelly and Prince Rainier of Monaco

Hollywood royalty Grace Kelly became actual royalty in 1956 after saying "I do" to Prince Rainier of Monaco. The 40-minute ceremony was broadcast across Europe, watched by millions and attended by over 600 guests. The couple had three children, Caroline, Albert and Stephanie, but the union put an end to Kelly's glittering screen career.

Prince Charles and Princess Diana

Prince Charles and Lady Diana Spencer married in St Paul's Cathedral on July 29th, 1981. Millions watched the elaborate ceremony on television, while an additional half a million lined the streets of London to mark the occasion. 20-year-old Diana was the first English woman in 300 years to marry a British heir to the throne, and produced two sons, William and Harry. Sadly, the fairytale was not to last – by 1996 the couple had divorced. Diana later called her wedding day "the worst day of my life".

Prince Andrew and Sarah Ferguson

Prince Andrew married childhood acquaintance Sarah Ferguson at Westminster Abbey on 23rd July 1986. Although the couple initially appeared to enjoy a happy marriage – quickly producing two daughters, Beatrice and Eugenie – by 1992 they were announcing their separation. Despite the subsequent release of tabloid photographs depicting "Fergie" in a compromising situation with her financial advisor, she and Andrew eventually parted on amicable terms. Their split was finalized in 1996.

“**Love** is the **golden** thread that ties our **hearts** and **souls** together.”

Mother Teresa

Tattoos

Tattoos as fashion statements are an increasingly common sight nowadays, and tattooed declarations of love are quickly gaining in popularity. We've all heard horror stories of young lovers permanently etching his or her beloved's name upon their person, only to find themselves single five minutes later – so thank goodness this lady opted to display her love for something far more trustworthy: Irish boyband Westlife!

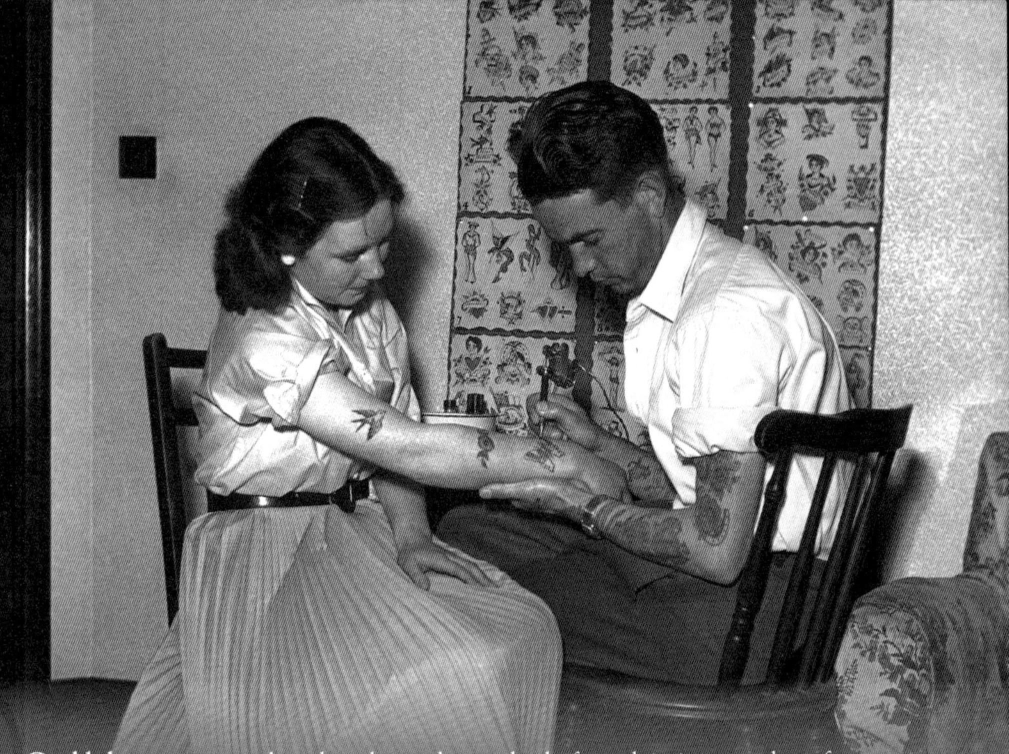

Could there – just maybe – be a less risky method of proclaiming your love for someone? If there is, somebody needs to tell the celebrities of this world: who could forget Johnny Depp's Winona Ryder arm-tribute, "Winona Forever" (later altered to read "Wino Forever")? Or David Beckham's misspelled Hindi tattoo, which reportedly translates as "Vhictoria"? Then there's Pete Doherty's "K in a heart" for ex-girlfriend Kate Moss, Katie Price's "Peter" wrist tattoo… just think carefully before going under the needle!

It's never too
early for love.

The cartoon world is packed with famous couples – who could forget these iconic pairs?

Aladdin and Jasmine
Ariel and Eric
Beauty and The Beast
Beavis and Butt-head
Bianca and Bernard
Charlie Brown and Lucy
Cinderella and Prince Charming
Donald Duck and Daisy Duck
Fred and Wilma Flinstone
Hercules and Megara
Homer and Marge Simpson
Lady and The Tramp
Mickey Mouse and Minnie Mouse
Peter Pan and Wendy
Pocahontas and John Smith
Popeye and Olive Oyl
Quasimodo and Esmeralda
Ren and Stimpy
Rocky and Bullwinkle
Scooby-Doo and Shaggy
Simba and Nala
Sleeping Beauty and Prince Philip
Tarzan and Jane
Tom and Jerry
Tweety Pie and Sylvester
Yogi Bear and Boo Boo
Dangermouse and Penfold

Answers to the Love Quiz 1 (page 61)

Matching the famous lovers

Romeo and Juliet	Scarlett O'Hara and Rhett Butler
Cleopatra and MarkAnthony	Jane Eyre and Rochester
Lancelot and Guinevere	Judy Finnigan and Richard Madeley
Tristan and Isolde	John Lennon and Yoko Ono
Paris and Helen	Pyramus and Thisbe
Orpheus and Eurydice	Elizabeth Bennett and Mr Darcy
Napoleon and Josephine	Shah Jahan and Mumtaz Mahal
Odysseus and Penelope	Marie and Pierre Curie
Melanie Griffith and Antonio Banderas	Queen Victoria and Prince Albert

Answers to the Love Quiz 2 (page 138)

1. 2003
2. Prince
3. Tom Cruise, about Katie Holmes
4. 4 months
5. Donna Summer
6. 1,579 metres
7. They all married at the Little White Wedding Chapel in Vegas. Geldof to Paula Yates, Spears to Jason Alexander, Collins to Peter Holm and Willis to Demi Moore
8. They were the first gay couple in the UK to have a civil partnership
9. 60,000
10. The Wizard of Oz

And finally...

ALL
LOVE
L'AMOUR
IHR
LO
IS
C'EST
BRAUCHT
QUE
YOU
POUR
ALS
NEED
VOUS